I Can Do It All By Myself
books by
Shigeo Watanabe

How do I put it on?

What a good lunch!

Get set! Go!

I'm the king of the castle!

I can ride it!

Where's my daddy?

I can build a house!

I can take a walk!

Text copyright © 1977 by Shigeo Watanabe.
Illustrations copyright © 1977 by Yasuo Ohtomo.
English text © 1979 by The Bodley Head.
All rights reserved.
Published in the United States by Philomel Books, a division of
The Putnam Publishing Group, 51 Madison Ave., New York, N.Y. 10010.
Printed in Hong Kong
Library of Congress CIP information at back of book.

an I CAN DO IT ALL BY MYSELF book

How do I put it on?

Story by Shigeo Watanabe   Pictures by Yasuo Ohtomo

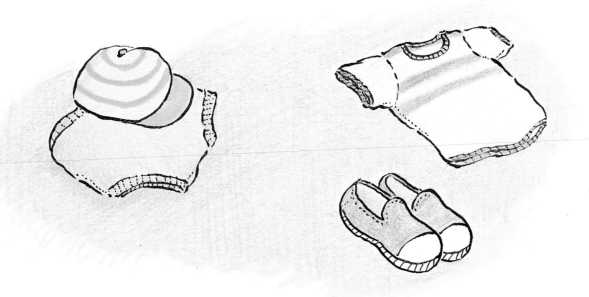

GETTING DRESSED

PHILOMEL BOOKS

I can get dressed all by myself.

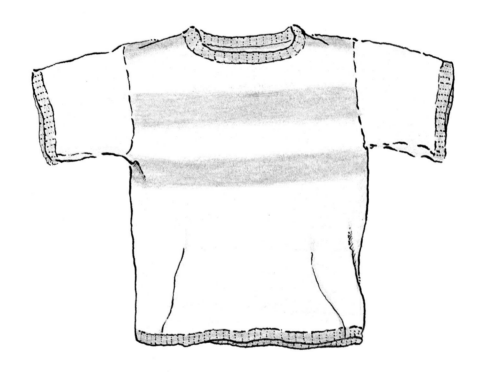

This is my shirt.

Do I put it on like this?

No!

I put my shirt over my head.

These are my pants.

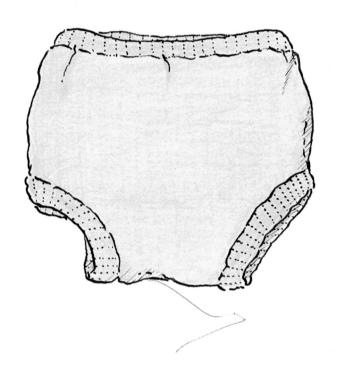

Do I put them on like this?

No!

I put my legs through my pants.

This is my cap.

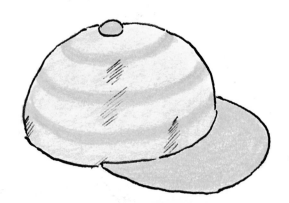

Do I put it on like this?

No!

I put my cap on my head.

These are my shoes.

Do I put them on like this?

No!

I put my shoes on my feet.

Here goes . . .

Shirt.

Pants.

Cap.

Shoes.

I'm ready. Off I go!

I got dressed all by myself.

Library of Congress Cataloging in Publication Data
Watanabe, Shigeo, 1928-   How do I put it on?
(An I can do it all by myself book)
SUMMARY: A bear demonstrates the right and wrong ways
to put on shirt, pants, cap, and shoes.
[1. Clothing and dress—Fiction] I. Ohtomo, Yasuo. II. Title.
PZ7.W2615Ho   [E]   79-12714
ISBN 0-399-20761-9
ISBN 0-399-21040-7 pbk.
First paperback edition published in 1984.
Fifth impression.